The Three Billy Goats Gruff

Miles Kelly

Once there lived three billy goats gruff. They loved nothing more than eating grass all day long.

Munch!

Munch! Munch!

But it had to be the sweetest, tastiest grass they could find.

"Time to look for some tastier grass," said the big billy goat gruff to his brothers one day. So they set off along the river.

They wandered for miles and miles.
"Are we there yet?"
asked the littlest billy goat gruff.
"I'm starving!"

At last they came to a bridge, and on the other side of it they saw a lush meadow. "That looks delicious!" said the littlest billy goat gruff.

"Yummy!" agreed his brothers.

But a nasty troll
lived under the bridge. He had long,
sharp claws and pointed teeth. He liked
nothing better than goat for dinner.

Trip trap, trip trap!

"I'll cross first," said the littlest billy goat gruff. And off he trotted with a trip trap, trip trap, over the wooden bridge.

Suddenly the troll jumped out in front of him. "Who is trip-trapping over MY BRIDGE?" he roared.

"Only me," said the littlest billy goat gruff. "I need to get to the meadow beyond."

"Stop!" growled the troll.

"I'm going to eat you for my dinner!"

"Oh, but you should wait until my brother comes along," said the littlest billy goat gruff. "He's FAR bigger than me."

"Byeee!"

And with a hop and a skip, the little goat jumped into the meadow beyond.

Not long after, the middle-sized billy goat gruff crossed the bridge. Trip trap, trip trap!

"STOP RIGHT THERE!" the troll roared, jumping out. "Who is trip-trapping over MY BRIDGE?"

"It's me, looking for tasty grass to eat," said the middle-sized billy goat gruff.

"But I want you for
my dinner,"
said the troll.

"Oh, wait for my big brother – he'll make a much better meal," said the middle-sized billy goat gruff. And with a hop and a skip, he jumped into the meadow.

The biggest
billy goat gruff
was very strong with
long, sharp
horns. He decided
to cross the
bridge to join his
little brothers.

TRIP TRAP,
TRIP TRAP!
The big billy goat
gruff clattered over
the wooden bridge.

"That sounds like dinner!" said the troll. He grabbed his knife and fork and jumped out onto the bridge.

"Who is TRIP-TRAPPING over MY BRIDGE?" he roared.

"ME!" said the big billy goat gruff, coming face to face with the troll. "I'm on my way to the meadow beyond."

"But I want you for my dinner," said the troll a little nervously.

"I don't think so!" said the big billy goat gruff.

The big billy goat gruff lowered his head and showed the troll his long, sharp horns. He took a run at the troll and... BIFF!

Up went the troll high into the air, over the bridge and far into the river below. SPLASH!

"ARGGGH!"

TRIP TRAP, TRIP TRAP!

The big billy goat gruff clattered all the way over the bridge and jumped into the meadow beyond.

The three billy goats gruff
lived happily ever after.
They were never
bothered by
trolls again!